This dragon book bel

....

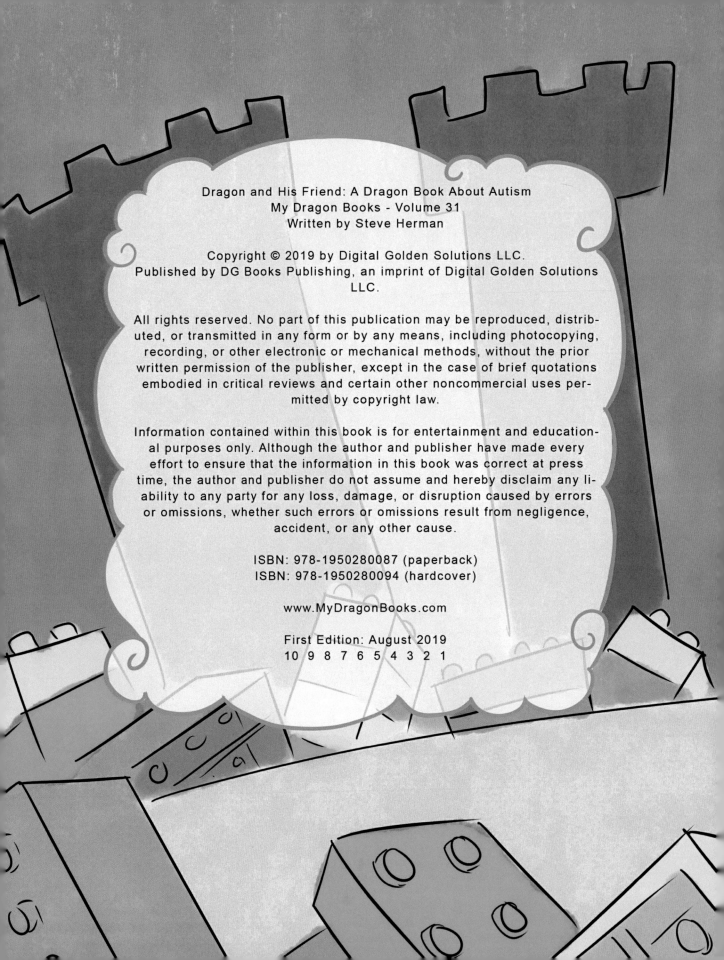

Dragon and His Friend: A Dragon Book About Autism
My Dragon Books - Volume 31
Written by Steve Herman

ISBN: 978-1950280087 (paperback)
ISBN: 978-1950280094 (hardcover)

www.MyDragonBooks.com

First Edition: August 2019
10 9 8 7 6 5 4 3 2 1

We hope you like our stories
and that you've been entertained
By reading all about the ways
a dragon must be trained.

Here's another story –
I assure you it's a dandy –
It teaches us a lesson
that may come in pretty handy!

A new kid came to Diggory's school
one day last September,
And Diggory learned a lesson
that he always will remember.

Teacher said his name was Michael,
but we just called him Mike;
Diggory Doo was sure
that Mike was someone he would like.

Whenever they were talking and not look him in the eye. It seemed like Mike was being rude, and Diggory wondered why.

HE'S KINDA RUDE.

WEEE!!!

That's not all that Diggory saw –
He noticed other things,
Sometimes Mike would flap his arms
as if they might be wings.

Diggory got his feelings hurt. He wondered, "Could it be... Since I have wings upon my back, he's making fun of me?!"

When Mike would play with building blocks, he didn't want to quit,

And if you tried to make him stop, he might throw a fit.

Once he built a rocket with an astronaut inside – Diggory Doo could never do that, even if he tried!

Once Diggory said, "Hey, Mike, time to put the toys away... So we can eat our lunch," but Mike still wished to play.

Mike got mad at Diggory Doo, and he refused to speak Or play with Diggory Doo at all 'til later on that week.

This was not just any mad –
No, this was something more.
Diggory'd never seen a mad
quite like this before.

But Diggory Doo soon noticed that Mike
brought his Teddy bear;
Since Diggory Doo could not bring his,
he thought it most unfair!

IT'S TIME TO GO.

I DON'T WANT TO!

Diggory Doo liked Mike, but he found it kind of strange That Mike would cry and get upset whenever things would change,

?

Like when teacher said, "It's time to go," or someone moved the toys –

SCREEEEEEEEEECH!!!

Mike also got quite startled when he heard a sudden noise.

"That makes sense," said Diggory Doo. "It might be the reason why... Mike sometimes wants to be alone or won't look me in the eye."

"Some folks are very talented and have amazing skills,"

"Like Mike does with his building blocks and the awesome things he builds!"

"He'll spend hours on a single task,
playing all alone;
He may become upset
when he must leave his *'comfort zone.'*"

"You have the same emotions,
but Mike may feel them stronger –
Like you, he'll be okay,
but it may take a little longer."

Diggory Doo was catching on;
he seemed to comprehend.
"Let's talk about some ways,"
I said, "to be a better friend."

"Although change is normal,
it can make Mike feel distressed;
Be thoughtful of his feelings,
and try to do your best."

"When Mike is feeling angry,
you may find it is the case
That the best way you can help
is to give him time and space."

"Maybe you can teach him how you learned to count to ten Whenever you are angry and how helpful that has been!"

"Your friend is kind of quiet and shy,
and hard to get to know,
But so were you, Diggory Doo,
not so long ago."

Now Mike and Diggory Doo are friends –
It matters not one bit
That the two of them are different –
They're still a perfect fit!

We may not look and act the same;
still this much is true –
**Everyone needs love
and a friend to help them through.**

Besides, if we were just the same,
how dull the world would be!
Just learn from Mike and Diggory Doo!
Embrace diversity!

Get your FREE gift
from Diggory Doo at
www.MyDragonBooks.com/gift